ABC
and
counting

Illustrated by Gill Guile and Text
Design by Desmond Marwood

© 2005 Brown Watson, England
Reprinted 2006 (twice), 2007 (twice), 2009, 2010

Brown Watson
ENGLAND

Aa

WHAT IS AN ANIMAL?

An animal is a living thing that is able to move and feel. Here are some different sorts of animals.

Can you find these animals in the other pages of this book?

animal

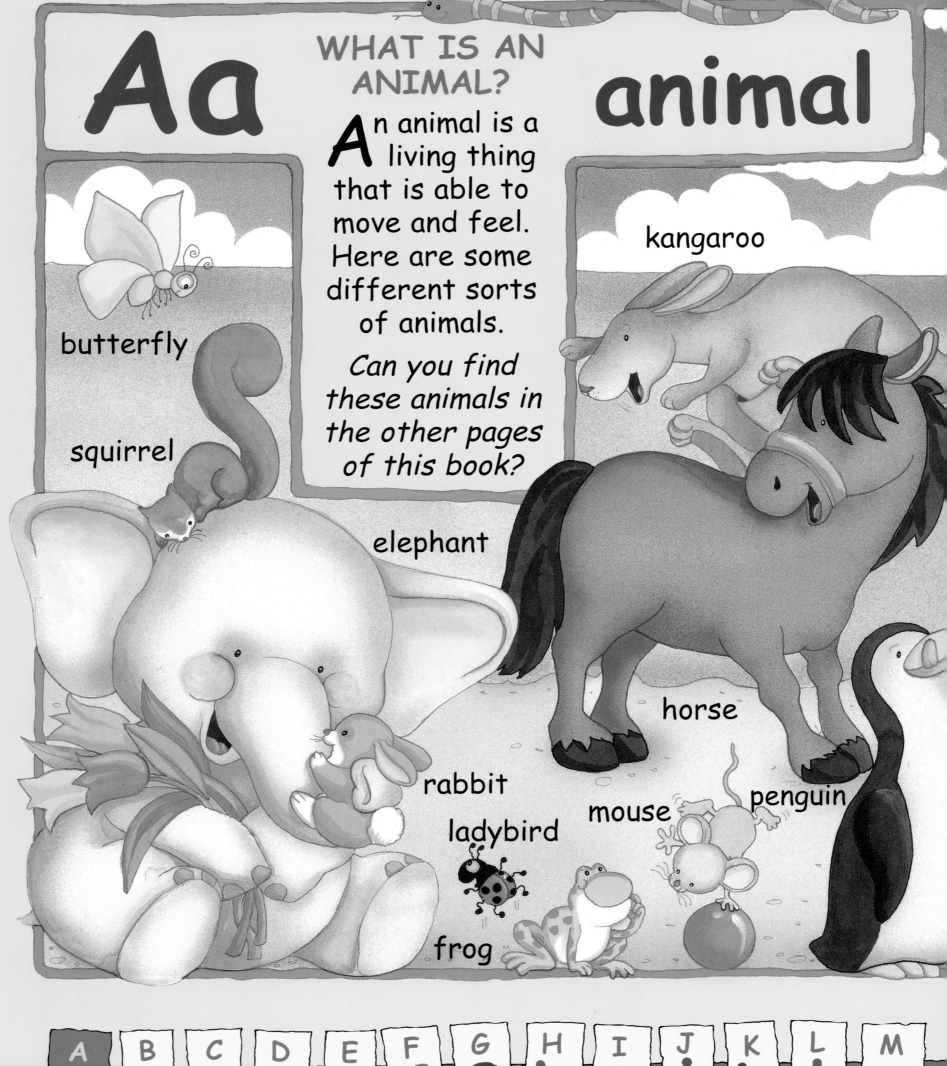

butterfly

squirrel

elephant

kangaroo

horse

rabbit

ladybird

mouse

penguin

frog

A B C D E F G H I J K L M
a b c d e f g h i j k l m

whale

giraffe

zebra

tortoise

octopus

N O P Q R S T U V W X Y Z
n o p q r s t u v w x y z

Bb  butterfly

THE BUTTERFLY'S BEAUTY SLEEP

The beetle's friend was a caterpillar who fell asleep for many years. A shell grew around the caterpillar's body and the beetle thought he would never see his friend again. Then, one day, the shell around the caterpillar cracked and out stepped a beautiful butterfly.

"Yes, it really is me!" the butterfly told the beetle. "Did I never tell you about the magic beauty sleep that turns caterpillars into butterflies?"

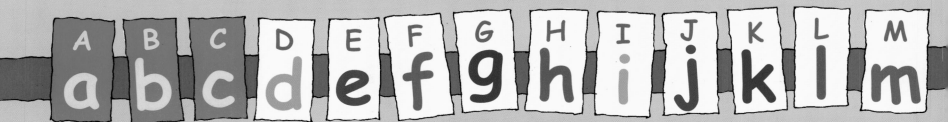

Cc

cat

THE CAT WHO VISITED THE QUEEN

A cat went to London to visit the Queen. "Mummy!" cried her baby kittens when she got back home. "Tell us about your day!" Mother cat told how she had frightened away a mouse from beneath the Queen's chair. The Queen was so pleased that she told Mother cat to bring the kittens with her on her next visit. The kittens are now looking forward to meeting the Queen.

N O P Q R S T U V W X Y Z

n o p q r s t u v w x y z

Dd dog

DANNY THE DOG AND HIS BONE

Danny the dog could not find his bone. The rabbit could not help Danny find his bone. The squirrels had not seen his bone. The birds didn't know where to look for Danny's bone. But, the cat was smiling because she had hidden Danny's bone and knew where it was.

Can you see where the cat has hidden Danny's bone?

A B C D E F G H I J K L M
a b c d e f g h i j k l m

E e  elephant

ELSIE'S SKIP IN THE PARK

Elsie the Elephant's two aunties took her to play in the park. "I wish I'd brought my skipping rope," said Elsie. "Elephants don't need skipping ropes!" laughed Aunt Edna. "We've all got skipping trunks!" laughed Aunt Elizabeth. Then, they held each other's trunks and swung them all around, so that Elsie could skip in the middle of them. What fun she had!

N O P Q R S T U V W X Y Z

n o p q r s t u v w x y z

F f   frog

FROGS THAT CROAK IN THE NIGHT

Three frogs lived in a pond. The big frog croaked: "Croak! Croak!" The middle frog croaked: "Creak! Creak!" and the little frog croaked: "Crick! Crick!" When they all croaked together, they made quite a pleasant chorus. So, every moonlit evening, the three frogs sat on water lily leaves and sang for the king of the goldfish pond and the royal members of his court.

A B C D E F G H I J K L M
a b c d e f g h i j k l m

N O P Q R S T U V W X Y Z

n o p q r s t u v w x y z

Gg giraffe

FOOD FROM THE TOP SHELF

As well as eating grass, many wild animals began feeding on the fruit and leaves of bushes and shrubs. Soon, there was hardly enough food for all of the animal kingdom. So, the giraffe grew its long, long neck to reach high up into the tree-tops for the food other animals could not reach. "Yummie!" said George Giraffe. "The food tastes nice and fresh up here."

A B C D E F G H I J K L M
a b c d e f g h i j k l m

Hh
horse

HARRY'S FAVOURITE DAY

Harry the horse's working life was over and now he lived in a field of his own. Schooldays were his favourite days, because children passing his field would often stop to fuss him or give him a sandwich from their lunchbox. Sometimes they even gave him a lovely red apple!

N O P Q R S T U V W X Y Z

n o p q r s t u v w x y z

Ii

insect

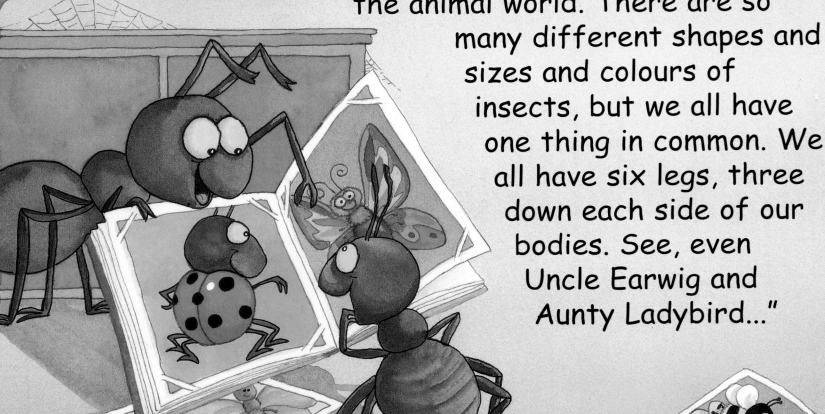

THE BIGGEST FAMILY IN THE WORLD!

"**W**hat's this old book?" asked Alfie Ant as he pulled it from the back of a dusty old cupboard. It was full of pictures of different sorts of insects. "That's our Insect Family Photo Album," Mother Ant told him. "Ants like us belong to the insect family. It's the biggest family in the animal world. There are so many different shapes and sizes and colours of insects, but we all have one thing in common. We all have six legs, three down each side of our bodies. See, even Uncle Earwig and Aunty Ladybird..."

A B C D E F G H I J K L M
a b c d e f g h i j k l m

Jj jackdaw

THE FLYING THIEF

The jackdaw birds flew over Katie Kitten. Their greedy eyes looked at the diamond ring Katie's owner had fastened to her collar. It sparkled brightly in the sunlight.

One day, the sparkling ring was missing. "It must have dropped off on the lawn," sobbed Katie. Mother Cat told Katie how jackdaw birds often stole shiny objects. When the jackdaws were away, Katie climbed up the mulberry tree and, sure enough, found the ring tucked away in the corner of their nest!

N O P Q R S T U V W X Y Z
n o p q r s t u v w x y z

Kk kangaroo

KANGAROO'S SPORTS DAY

With the help of big, strong legs and a powerful tail, the kangaroo always won lots of prizes at the Animal Annual Sports Day. With a hop, a skip and a thump of his tail, the bouncy kangaroo took off from the ground. The kangaroo flew high up into the air above the other animals to win the high jump.

A B C D E F G H I J K L M
a b c d e f g h i j k l m

Next, the kangaroo gave another hop, skip and a thump of its tail to win the long jump!

Then finally...

...the kangaroo made lots of little bounces and won the hurdle race!

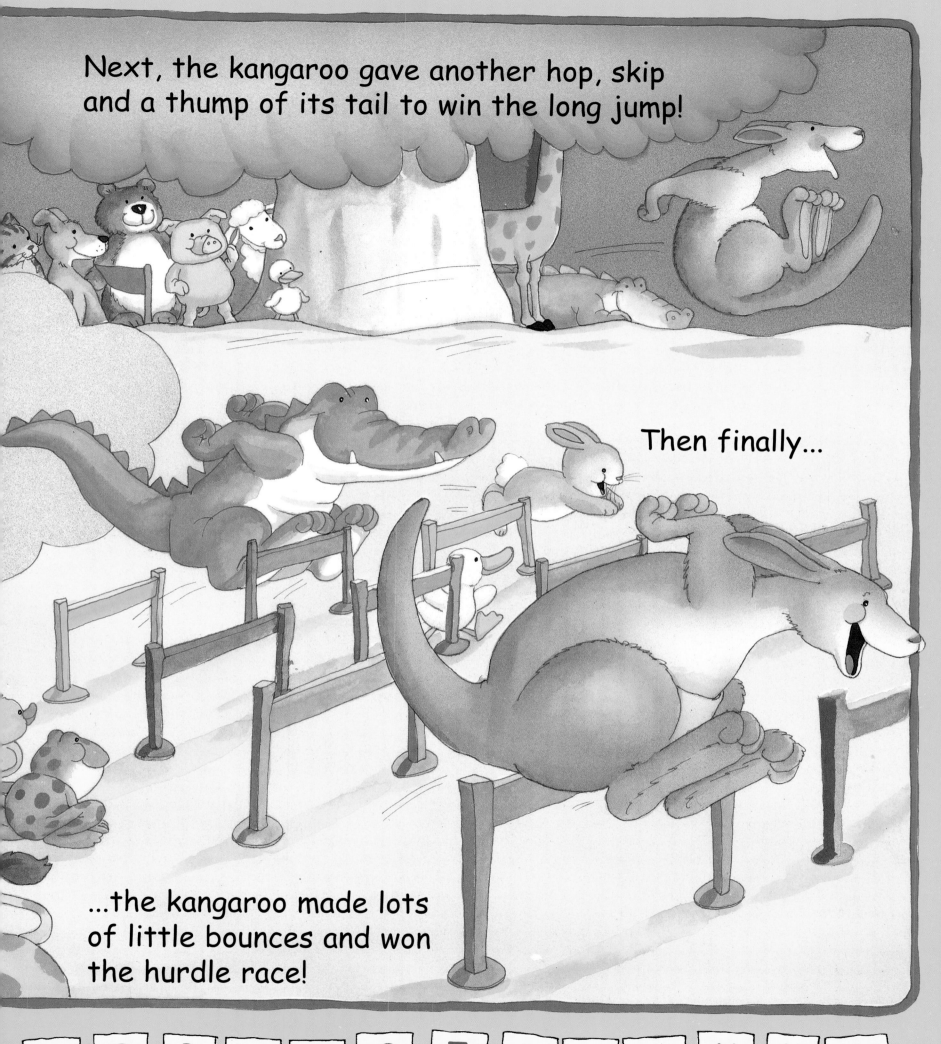

N O P Q R S T U V W X Y Z
n o p q r s t u v w x y z

Ll ladybird

LADYBIRD AND HER SPOTS

"Ladybirds should be bright red without any ugly black spots," Ladybird told her friend, Beetle. "Just imagine how beautiful I'd look if I was bright red all over." Beetle agreed to paint out Ladybird's black spots. Then, Ladybird suddenly cried: "Ouch!" and jumped back from the peck of a big blackbird.

"Oh, sorry, Ladybird," said the blackbird. "Without your black spots I thought you were a bright red berry, ready for eating."

A a B b C c D d E e F f G g H h I i J j K k L l M m

Mm mouse

HAPPY BIRTHDAY MONTY MOUSE

"Happy Birthday, Monty Mouse!" cried Mother Mouse. "Here's your favourite breakfast of muffins with maple syrup." But Monty was too interested in his pile of presents and birthday cards to feel hungry. There was a model plane from Mum and Dad and a computer game from his sister, Mary. Grandma and Grandad had sent him money, because they knew he felt like a grown-up if he went to the shop by himself to choose his own present.

N O P Q R S T U V W X Y Z
n o p q r s t u v w x y z

Nn
nightingale

SWEET SONG OF KINDNESS

The nightingale sings the sweetest song of all birds. Once upon a time, the Emperor of China had a pet nightingale. Each evening he fed the bird in its cage and in return the nightingale sang a song for him. Then, one day, someone left the cage door open and the bird flew away. The Emperor was broken-hearted, but the nightingale returned and told him: "You cared for me very well, so I will return each evening and sing a special song for you."

A B C D E F G H I J K L M
a b c d e f g h i j k l m

Oo octopus

MANY HANDS MAKE LIGHT WORK

"We just don't know how you keep your home so tidy," Mrs. Shark told Mrs. Octopus when all the fish wives met for coffee. "I just can't get home help," moaned Mrs. Cod. "Servants are so hard to find," croaked Mrs. Whiting. Of course, they had all forgotten that Mrs. Octopus had eight long legs, or arms, with suckers to hold things firmly. She was able to dust, wash dishes and do all sorts of other things at the same time!

N O P Q R S T U V W X Y Z
n o p q r s t u v w x y z

Pp
penguin

PENGUIN PARTY

Polly and Peter Penguin were getting ready to go to a party. Pamela Penguin arrived to look after their egg while they were out. She put the penguin egg between her feet to keep it warm. Peter took a long time choosing his tie. Do you think he chose the right one?

They enjoyed the party very much indeed!

A B C D E F G H I J K L M
a b c d e f g h i j k l m

Qq   queen

LONG LIVE THE QUEEN!

There was great rejoicing throughout the Land of the Beehive, where Good Queen Bee ruled over thousands of bees.

The time had come for the Queen and an army of her most faithful workers to leave the hive and fly off to build a new palace in some distant land.

A great feast was held and thousands of bees cried: "Good Luck, Your Majesty!" as the Queen and her workers flew off into the sunshine.

N O P Q R S T U V W X Y Z
n o p q r s t u v w x y z

Rr  rabbit

RABBIT'S PUZZLE HOME

The postman told Roger Rabbit that he had so many front doors, he never knew which letter box to pop the letters through. "Oh, any door will do," laughed Roger. "My home is such a mess. I dig out tunnels, or burrows as we call them, and they go this way and that way. Sometimes, I don't know where I am myself."

Can you find your way through Roger's home and out of his back door?

A B C D E F G H I J K L M
a b c d e f g h i j k l m

N O P Q R S T U V W X Y Z
n o p q r s t u v w x y z

Ss squirrel

MOTHER SQUIRREL'S MISSING NUTS

"I'm so hungry, I could eat a whole walnut tree," cried one young squirrel. Mother Squirrel was going to make her family a special nut soup for dinner, but she could not remember where she had put the bags of nuts for safe-keeping.

Can you see where Mother Squirrel put four bags of nuts for safe-keeping?

A B C D E F G H I J K L M
a b c d e f g h i j k l m

Tt tortoise

THE RACING TORTOISE

Some animals laughed at Thomas Tortoise because he moved so slowly. "Well," he told them, "I was the tortoise that once beat a hare in a running race!" After that, the animals treated Thomas very politely. They did not know he was so famous! "Im not telling them," smiled Thomas to himself, "that during the race the hare was so far ahead he lay down for a rest. I tip-toed past him to the winning post while he was fast asleep!"

N O P Q R S T U V W X Y Z

n o p q r s t u v w x y z

Uu unicorn

THE UNICORN AND THE LION

Long ago, lived an animal called a unicorn. It looked like a beautiful white horse with a long horn growing from its forehead. It was brave and had magical powers and many believed it should be King of the Animals. But, the golden-bearded lion was already King. Three times the unicorn fought the lion for his crown and lost. Finally, because the unicorn had fought so bravely, the lion gave him a golden neckband, decorated with small crowns, and a part of his kingdom to rule over.

A B C D E F G H I J K L M

a b c d e f g h i j k l m

Vv

vet

A SPECIAL ANIMAL DOCTOR

Vet is our short name for a veterinary doctor. Vets are special doctors who care for animals when they are hurt, or poorly. This farmer has sent for the vet because his cow is poorly. The vet is giving the cow an injection.

The vet has given some tablets to the sick pig.

The vet has put a bandage over a cut on the dog's leg.

N O P Q R S T U V W X Y Z
n o p q r s t u v w x y z

Ww 🐋 whale

A WHALE OF A TIME!

Walter Whale floated on the sunlit sea and watched the monkeys in their little boat. "Have you seen Pleasure Island?" the monkeys asked Walter. "We're going there for a picnic". Walter told them Pleasure Island was miles away, but if they liked they could hop up and picnic on his back. That's what the monkeys did. They shared their goodies and lemonade with Walter and they all had a lovely time.

A B C D E F G H I J K L M
a b c d e f g h i j k l m

Xx  x-ray

LOOKING INSIDE ANIMALS

When an animal is not well, the vet sometimes takes a special photograph called an X-ray. This helps him to see inside the animal, beneath its fur, feathers or skin. The bones of an animal can be seen clearly on an X-ray photograph.

The vet is looking at the X-ray of a horse.

This is an X-ray of a fish.   This is an X-ray of a bird.

Yy
young

YOUNG ANIMAL NAMES

Young or baby animals often have special names until they grow up to be like their parents. This young zebra is still with its mother. It is called a foal.

Here are some other animals and the names of their young ones...
kangaroo (joey)
pig (piglet)
cat (kitten)

A B C D E F G H I J K L M
a b c d e f g h i j k l m

duck (duckling)
lion (cub)
elephant (calf)
dog (puppy)
sheep (lamb)
hen (chick)
cow (calf)

N O P Q R S T U V W X Y Z
n o p q r s t u v w x y z

Zz 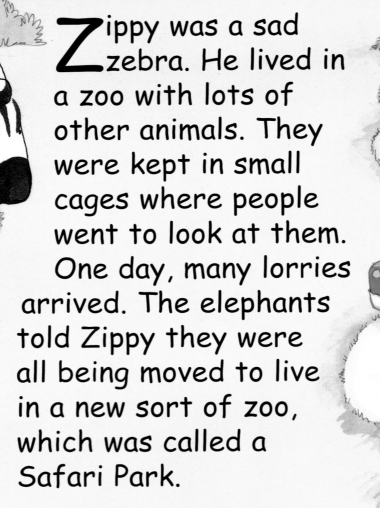 zebra

MOVING TO A NEW ZOO

Zippy was a sad zebra. He lived in a zoo with lots of other animals. They were kept in small cages where people went to look at them. One day, many lorries arrived. The elephants told Zippy they were all being moved to live in a new sort of zoo, which was called a Safari Park.

Life was a lot more fun for Zippy and his friends at the Safari Park.

A	B	C	D	E	F	G	H	I	J	K	L	M
a	b	c	d	e	f	g	h	i	j	k	l	m

As the alphabet animals say goodbye,
On a magic carpet off we fly,
Over the fields to a little barn,
To do some counting on the farm.

Have lots of fun!

N O P Q R S T U V W X Y Z
n o p q r s t u v w x y z

One dog

His name is Bob and he looks after the sheep on the farm.

The farmer was very cross because Bob had lost the sheep and didn't know where to find them.
"Off you go," the farmer told Bob, "and don't come back without the sheep. There are ten sheep altogether. You'll find them somewhere on the farm."

one two three four five six seven eight nine ten

Two farm horses

These horses work hard on the farm, but today the farmer has given them a day off.

Bob asked the two horses if they
had seen the sheep. They shook their heads and
told him he should ask the three cows in the
next field. Bob thanked the horses for their help
and ran off to ask the cows if they had seen the sheep.

1	2	3	4	5	6	7	8	9	10
one	two	three	four	five	six	seven	eight	nine	ten

Three cows

3
three

Cows spend a lot of their time munching grass.
This helps them to make the milk we drink.

The three cows didn't have many visitors to their field, so they made a fuss of Bob when he arrived. They were sorry they had not seen the sheep and suggested he asked the four goats in the next field. "They often mix with the sheep," mooed a cow.

one   two   three   four   five   six   seven   eight   nine   ten

Four goats

The four goats live in a field but go into their own special shed at night.

None of the four goats had seen Bob's sheep.
"I'm very glad they're not here," one goat told Bob.
"They keep us awake at night calling out 'Baa!
Baa!' to each other," another goat told Bob.
The goats said Bob should ask the pigs.

one two three four five six seven eight nine ten

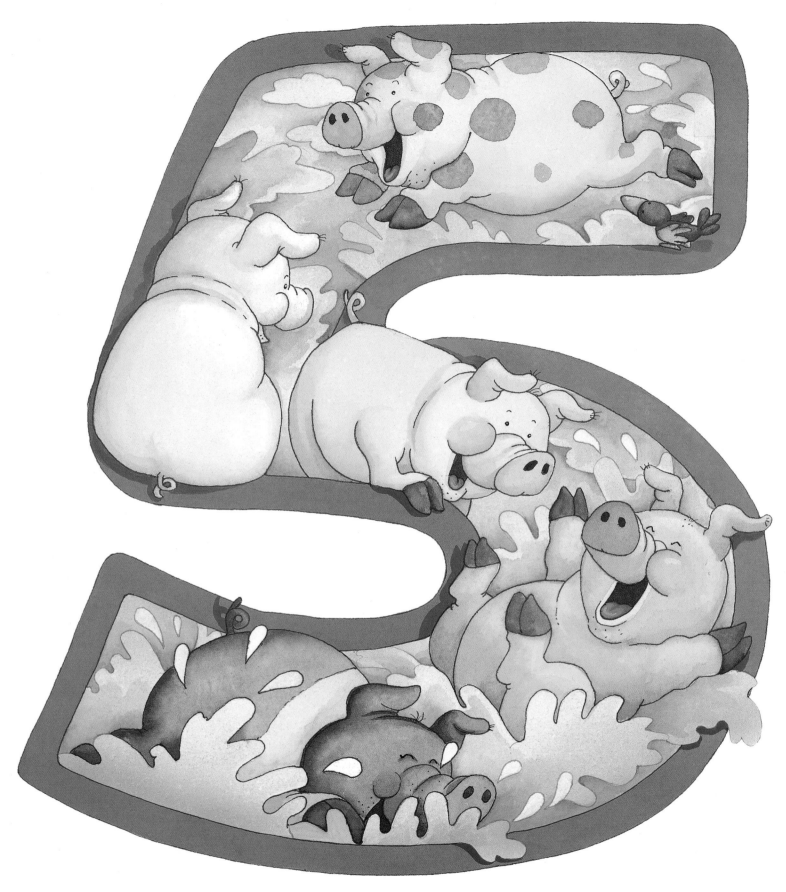

Five pigs

Most pigs are pinky-white, some are black and others have black patches or black spots.

The five pigs lived in a place called a pigsty.
They came up to the wall of their sty to speak
to Bob, but none of them had seen the sheep.
"Go and ask the rabbits," they grunted. "They see
everything going on as they nibble their lettuce."

one two three four five six seven eight nine ten

Six rabbits

The farmer keeps pet rabbits for his children to play with. Pet rabbits live in rabbit hutches.

Bob found the rabbits in their run outside the hutch. They told Bob they'd been too busy eating lettuce to have seen his sheep. They told him he should ask the farmyard cat's kittens. "They run all over the place," the rabbits told Bob. "They see everything!"

one   two   three   four   five   six   seven   eight   nine   ten

Seven kittens

7
seven

A kitten is a baby cat. These kittens are brothers and sisters. Their mother is the farmyard cat.

The kittens were full of mischief. They wanted
to play games with Bob. He thought they were all
a bit silly. They hadn't seen his sheep anyway, so Bob
just ran off to find the hens. "Mrs. Brown Hen is
very wise and is sure to help," barked Bob.

one　　two　　three　　four　　five　　six　　seven　　eight　　nine　　ten

eight

Eight hens
Like many other farm animals,
hens can be different colours and sizes.

Bob had been right to think Mrs. Brown Hen would be able to help him. Down by the pond, she had heard Mrs. Duck's baby ducklings talking about the sheep. "The baby ducklings will know where your sheep can be found," Mrs. Brown Hen told Bob.

one   two   three   four   five   six   seven   eight   nine   ten

Nine ducklings

A duckling is a baby duck. These are all sisters
and brothers and their mother is Mrs. Duck.

Bob found the ducklings with Mrs. Duck,
splashing about in the pond. Bob thought the ducklings
were even more playful than the kittens – and
much more noisy, too! "Yes!" they quacked to Bob.
"You'll find your sheep in the very next field."

one   two   three   four   five   six   seven   eight   nine   ten

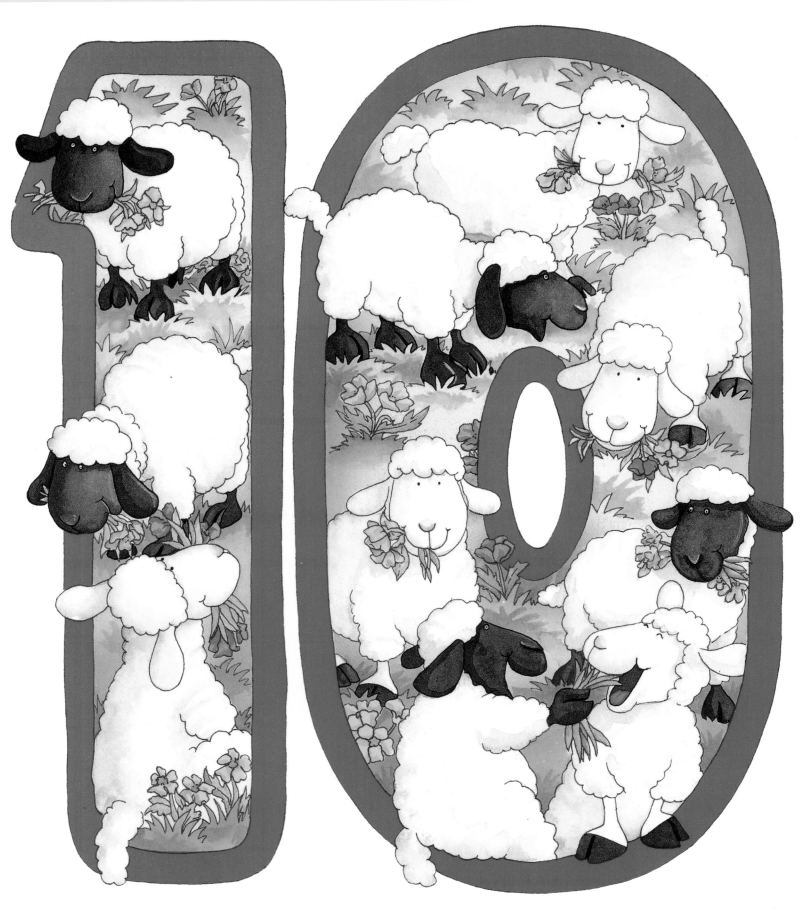

Ten sheep

Sheep have thick woolly coats. They are happy living outdoors and eating grass all day.

Bob had to rub his eyes when he got into the next field. The sheep were nowhere to be seen. Bob didn't know the sheep were playing a trick on him.
They were in the field, but they were all hiding.
Can you see where each of the ten sheep is hiding?

one   two   three   four   five   six   seven   eight   nine   ten

Suddenly, the sheep ran out from their hiding places. "Baa! Baa!" they cried as they chased each other in circles around Bob. The birds and the rabbits and all the other countryside animals thought it was such a funny sight.

Bob didn't think it was very funny. The sheep
ran round and round him so quickly that it
made him feel quite dizzy. He couldn't count the
sheep properly to see if they were all there.
Can you count them and see if there are ten sheep?

When the farmer counted them, there were not ten sheep. There were only nine. "One sheep is still missing," the farmer told Bob. "Off you go and find it." Can you help Bob find the way to the lost sheep?

Bob found the way to the lost sheep.
He took it back to the farmer.
The farmer added the one sheep
to the nine sheep so
that once again he had
all ten of his sheep.

Count them all to make
sure the farmer now
has his ten sheep.

The farmer told Bob he must practise counting.
He sent him to count the eggs in the henhouse.

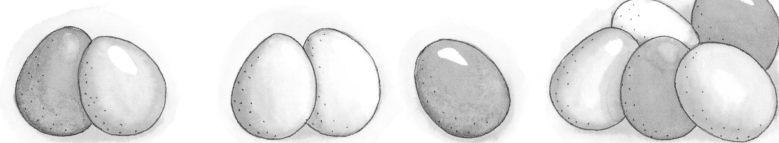

Two eggs and **two eggs** and **one egg** make **five eggs**

2 + 2 + 1 = 5

The farmer sent Bob to count the cows in the field.

One cow and **one cow** and **one cow** make **three cows**

1 + 1 + 1 = 3

Bob then had to count all the rabbits.

Three rabbits and **two rabbits** and **one rabbit** make **six rabbits**

3 + 2 + 1 = 6

Then, Bob counted all the cats on the farm.

Three cats and **two cats** and **two cats** make **seven cats**

3 + 2 + 2 = 7

Bob counted up all the hens.

Four hens and **three hens** and **one hen** make **eight hens**

4 + 3 + 1 = 8

Finally, Bob counted the ducks on the pond.

Five ducks and **two ducks** and **two ducks** make **nine ducks**

5 + 2 + 2 = 9

Here is a picture of the farmer outside his farmhouse. His dog, Bob, is running up the lane to the farm. You can also see all the other farm animals.

Count up all the farm animals you can see in the picture.

10 sheep

8 hens

9 ducklings

2 horses

1 dog

5 pigs

6 rabbits

7 kittens

4 goats

3 cows

It was the end of the day's work on the farm. All the animals had been counted, fed and made safe for the night. The farmer lay back in his favourite chair and his children gathered around to listen to a story.

His wife was busy getting their meal ready. Bob the sheepdog was really hungry after his busy day rounding up the sheep. He was looking forward to settling down in his basket for the night. The kittens would be sleeping in the kitchen with him until they were older. He hoped they wouldn't get up to too much mischief during the night!

Look at the picture and answer the questions:-

What is the number on Bob's bowl?
Can you find the seven kittens in the picture?
What number channel is on the television screen?
How many flowers are in the vase on the window sill?
How many pictures can you see hanging on the walls?
Two little mice were not invited into the kitchen,
but they are waiting patiently for any titbits.
Can you see where they are hiding?

The farmer's children went to bed and the farmer and his wife went to bed. The farmer's family and all the animals were soon safe and fast asleep. Bob the sheepdog lay down in his basket. Before he went to sleep he remembered his busy day. He remembered...

two horses...
three cows...four goats...
five pigs...six rabbits...seven kittens...
eight hens...nine ducklings...and, of course,
ten sheep – including the one that got lost!

Just to make sure he hadn't made a mistake, he closed his eyes and counted the sheep all over again.

"One sheep...two sheep...three sheep... four sheep...five sh-e-e-p...s-i-x sh-e-e-p... s-e-v-e-n sh-e-e-p...zzzzzzzzz!"